A'niya
and Her Friend
in the

Closet

Dedication

This book is dedicated to all of my loved ones and to those who are young at heart and have that special imaginary friend only they can see and cherish for that moment.

A'niya
and Her Friend
in the
Closet

SANDRA BARNES

ASA PUBLISHING CORPORATION
AN INNOVATIVE OUTSOURCE BOOK PUBLISHING HYBRID

ASA Publishing Corporation
An Accredited Hybrid Publishing House with the BBB
www.asapublishingcorporation.com

1285 N. Telegraph Rd., 376, Monroe, Michigan 48162

Copyrights©2020 Sandra Barnes, (Realistic Writing Incorporation LLC) All Rights Reserved
Book Title: A'niya and Her Friend in the Closet
Date Published: 11.09.2020
Edition: 1, *Trade Paperback*
Book ID: ASAPCID2380819
ISBN: 978-1-946746-89-4
LCCN: Cataloging-in-Publication Data

This book was published in the United States of America.
Great State of Michigan

A'niya
and Her Friend
in the
Closet

SANDRA BARNES

INTRODUCTION

At the tender age of six years old with a mind as sharp as a whip, little A'niya had always loved spending time alone in her bedroom. One day, A'niya found a friend in her closet.

After A'niya returned from school one day, her grandma

decided to pay her a little visit. Going inside and walking toward

A'niya's bedroom door, her grandma can hear her talking to someone. Opening the door, to grandma's surprise, she finds her sitting on the floor playing with her little tea set all alone.

Grandma pausing for a few seconds, then asks, "A'niya, who are you talking with?"

"I was talking to my friend that lives in my closet," she replies.

With an amazed look, grandma walks over to the closet to see A'niya's friend.

Opening the door, she finds there is no one inside. A'niya then says to her grandma, "I think my friend left through the back of my closet." In awe, grandma reaches down, gives her a kiss on the forehead and then walks out of her bedroom.

The following day, grandma has a feeling A'niya may be stopping by to see her after school, so she begins to prepare the two of them a little snack.

Minutes later, the school bus arrives at grandma's house. A'niya jumps off the bus and runs toward the door where grandma invites her to come inside to sit down to eat.

With a smile on her face, Grandma asks, "What is the name of your friend in your closet?"

Grinning, she looked at her grandma and said, "He never told me his name." She then gets up from her chair, gives grandma a big kiss and leaves the house, skipping her little way home.

A few days later, after returning home from school, A'niya runs excitedly into grandma's house saying, "Tonight it's going to snow!"

Grandma stops what she's doing and invites A'niya to walk over to the door. Then she points to the sky and says, "Little one, it's too warm to snow. Also, there are no snow clouds."

A'niya, with a sad little look upon her face, turns and says, "I have to go home now." She leaves the house and heads home.

Hours later, it's almost the middle of the night when grandma's telephone rings. Grandma answers only to hear A'niya saying with such excitement in her voice, "I told you! I told you! Look out your window!"

Grandma asks, "Do you know how late it is? Now, why should I look out of my window at this time of night?"

A'niya replies, "Because it's really snowing, Grandma!"

Taking a look out of her window, Grandma sees that it is indeed actually snowing. "Wow! Amazing! How did you know, A'niya?"

A'niya says, "Grandma, you wouldn't believe it. While I was in my bed asleep, I was being shaken by my ghost friend to wake up and get out of bed. He said, "A'niya, you gotta get up and go take a look out your window!" So, I jumped out of bed and rushed over to see what's going on. That's when I saw the pretty snowflakes falling to the ground."

I was so excited that I ran down the hallway yelling for my

mom and dad to take me outside so I could make a snow angel, but they said I have to wait until morning.

Still bubbling with much excitement, A'niya decides to call her grandma back. "See Grandma, I really do have a friend that lives in my closet!"

-The End-

Conclusion

Anyone can have a special friend in their life if they only believe.

A'niya found her best friend in the comfort of her very own

bedroom.

About the Author

Sandra A. Barnes

Reared in a small town of North, South Carolina, where she attended North Elementary and North High School. She found her passion for writing at a very early age. She is an inspirational writer of realistic stories. She is the author of *Battered Beaten and Scorned Still I Rise Above It All (Book 1 of 2)*, and *Reflection of a Broken Butterfly*.

She is affiliated with the group women health studies, Marquis Who's Who.

www.ingramcontent.com/pod-product-compliance
Lightning Source LLC
Chambersburg PA
CBHW041544240626
47164CB00002B/118